ISBN 9798849774459

website www.healthhavenonline.com

email louise.dougherty@healthhavenonline.com

TO MY CHILDREN, DANNY, RYAN AND LAUREN WHO INSPIRED THESE STORIES AS WE LIVED OUR ADVENTURES

MR. WHETHERBY'S TEA PARTY

LOUISE DOUGHERTY

ON A SUNNY DAY WITH CLEAR BLUE SKIES, A SPARK LIT UP IN MR. WHETHERBY'S EYES.

IN HIS COZY HOME WITH A BEAUTIFUL GARDEN, HE'S SO POLITE, HE SAYS "I BEG YOUR PARDON."

HIS HOUSE IS SO NEAT, EVERYTHING IS IN ORDER. AROUND HIS WALLS, HE HAS A TURTLE BORDER.

THE TOWELS ARE FOLDED NEATLY, THE CUPS ARE IN THE CUPBOARD.
EVERYTHING IS JUST RIGHT, LIKE OLD MOTHER HUBBARD

WHAT SHOULD I DO ON THIS FINE DAY?
I WILL HAVE A PARTY, AND INVITE FRIENDS OVER TO PLAY.

WILL CALL MY FRIENDS ONE BY ONE.
I'LL MAKE TEA AND APPLE MUFFINS.
IT WILL BE FUN.

THE FIRST TO CALL IS MR. FROG.
CAN YOU COME TO A TEA PARTY?
WE'LL HAVE TEA AND APPLE
MUFFINS, AND IT WILL BE
HARDY.

IT SOUNDS ALRIGHT TO ME, BUT COULD WE HAVE BUG JUICE INSTEAD OF TEA?

Next on the list is Mr. Iguana. Please join my tea party, if you wanna.

"OK, but not in the yard. Can we sit inside if it's not too hard?" said Mr. Iguana.

NEXT TO BE CALLED WAS MR. SNAKE, PLEASE COME TO MY PARTY, APPLE MUFFINS I'LL BAKE,
"I'D LOVE TO, BUT IF IT'S NOT TOO MUCH TROUBLE, CAN YOU INSTEAD MAKE AN UPSIDE-DOWN APPLE BUBBLE?"

MR. WHETHERBY THOUGHT FOR A LONG TIME: HOW DID THIS GET SO OUT OF RHYME?
IT SEEMED TO BE A SIMPLE TEA PARTY, NOW IT'S OFF TO THE STORE, I CAN'T BE TARDY.

RUSH AND COOK THE MEAL TO PREPARE, WHO TO SIT HERE AND WHO TO SIT THERE,
NO PARTY OUTSIDE? MAKE BUG JUICE AND UPSIDE DOWN APPLE BUBBLE?

THIS ISN'T WHAT I PLANNED.
I THINK I'M IN TROUBLE.

NOW IT'S ALL DONE AND MY FRIENDS HAVE ARRIVED. WHY ARE WE SITTING HERE INSTEAD OF OUTSIDE?

NO, NO, IT'S BETTER OUTSIDE. NOW WHERE IS THE UPSIDE-DOWN APPLE BUBBLE NO ONE'S EVER TRIED?

HERE'S THE BUG JUICE,
BUT IT ENDED UP AS A
PUDDLE.
INSTEAD OF HAVING FUN, THEY
WERE GETTING INTO A MUDDLE.

THEY DIDN'T NOTICE THAT MR. WHETHERBY LOOKED SAD. THE UPSIDE-DOWN APPLE BUBBLE CAKE HAD BURNED, AND IT SMELLED REALLY BAD.

All the arguing continued until Mr. Whetherby walked outside.
The party was a flop, Mr. Whetherby cried.

THEN HE SAW THAT HIS TABLE WAS ALL SET IN HIS GARDEN. HE WAS SO POLITE HE SAID, "I BEG YOUR PARDON, BUT WOULD YOU LIKE TO HAVE APPLE MUFFINS AND TEA?" IT'S SUCH A BEAUTIFUL DAY, WON'T YOU JOIN ME?".

IT LOOKED SO DELICIOUS, THEY ALL SAT DOWN.
THE FRIENDS WERE ALL HAVING FUN; NOT A CONTRARY WORD COULD BE FOUND.

THEY DRANK TEA, ATE APPLE MUFFINS, LAUGHED, AND HAD A GREAT DAY.
WHEN THEY WERE FINISHED, THEY GOT UP TO PLAY.

IN THE END, IT TURNED OUT ALRIGHT.
THERE WASN'T ANY TEA
OR APPLE MUFFINS IN SIGHT.

PLEASE COME BACK TO PLAY
ANOTHER DAY.
THE PARTY WENT BETTER WHEN
HE DID IT HIS WAY.

WHEN MR. WHETHERBY WAS PUTTING HIS CUPS BACK ON THE SHELF,
HE REALIZED THAT TODAY HE HAD LEARNED TO THINK FOR HIMSELF.

Made in United States
North Haven, CT
25 November 2022

27231212R00015